For the magical staff and students of
Rock Creek Forest Elementary School —L.G.

This book is dedicated to two magical
creatures in my life, Rory and Robin. —A.Z.

Library of Congress Cataloging-in-Publication Data is available upon request.
ISBN 978-0-593-37625-6 (trade) — ISBN 978-0-593-37626-3 (lib. bdg.)
ISBN 978-0-593-37627-0 (ebook)

The illustrations were rendered in ink, scanned, and colored digitally.
The text of this book is set in 33-point Archer.
Interior design by Rachael Cole

MANUFACTURED IN CHINA
10 9 8 7 6 5 4 3 2 1
First Edition

Donut

The Unicorn Who Wants to Fly

Story by Laura Gehl ♥ Art by Andrea Zuill

RANDOM HOUSE STUDIO 🏠 NEW YORK

Donut jumps!

Donut thumps.

Donut jumps!

Donut flumps.

Donut slumps.

Donut sails!

Donut flails.

Donut wails.

Donut dreams.

Donut schemes.

Donut beams!

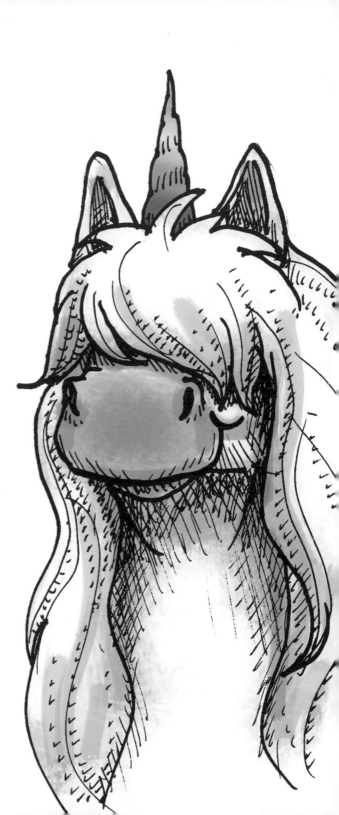

Donut tries.

Donut ties.

Donut flies!